Josie arrives at the Nursery to see Miss Hoolie.

"Morning, Josie!"

"Hiya, Miss Hoolie. Cute buggy! That reminds me, I'll be in charge of a whole load of buggies and prams later! I'm taking the Balamory Mums and Toddlers group to the Big City! We're off to Soft Play. The only thing is, I'm not sure exactly what happens there."

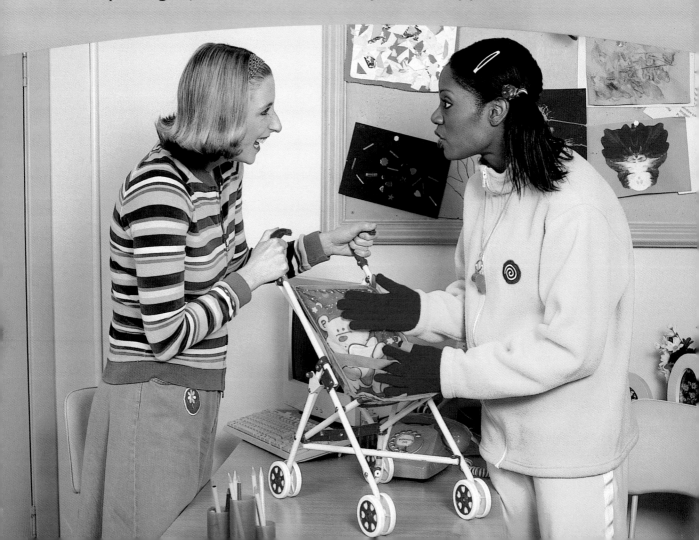

Balamory

BBC

Buggies and Prams

RED FOX

"Hello there! I'm Miss Hoolie! How are you? Today's a work day in Balamory. I wonder what adventures we'll get up to!"

Josie looks worried. "Spencer, your map is great, but it sounds like an obstacle course! How are we going to manage steps and bumpy streets and turnstiles with all those buggies and prams?"

"Maybe you need a different sort of map, Josie."

"I think I need a real map of the Big City. Now where will I find one of those? I know, I'll go and see Penny Pocket and Suzie Sweet," says Josie.

Josie arrives at the shop.

"Hi, Josie, what can we do for you today?" asks Penny.

"Well, I'm taking everyone to Soft Play in the Big City. Spencer has drawn me a fantastic map, but it's like an obstacle course! I have to find a different route for all the buggies and prams, so I need a real map of the Big City."

"We have just the map for you, Josie!" says Suzie.

Suzie unfolds a gigantic map, completely covering Penny!

"Hey!" comes a muffled voice.

"Ooops! Sorry, Penny!" laughs Suzie.

Suzie tries again, but this time she manages to cover Josie!

"Hey!" squeals Josie from underneath the huge map.

"Oh, sorry, Josie! Here, Penny, you hold this end . . . That's it."

"Right. Now, we start here . . ." explains Suzie.

"But that's the sea, Suzie!" Josie points out.

"Ah, yes, the blue bit, so it is! I know what we need . . ."

"A compass! To point you in the right direction, Josie. So, if this is south . . . and the wind is coming from the north . . ."

"Suzie! I'm going to Soft Play, not the North Pole!" laughs Josie.

"SUZIE!" Penny cries. "Josie is never going to get there at this rate! What you need, Josie, is a "wheel-friendly" route through the city. And I can help!"

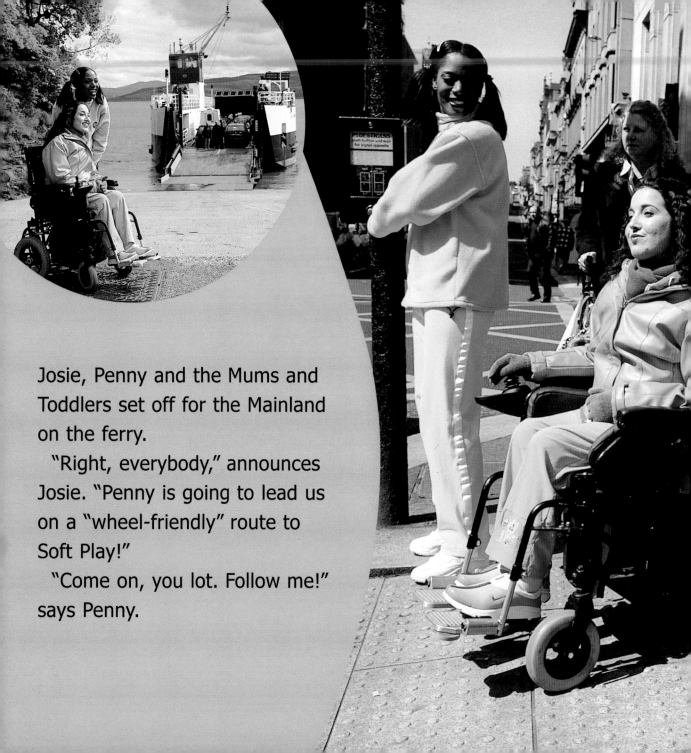

Josie, Penny and the Mums and Toddlers set off for the Mainland on the ferry.

"Right, everybody," announces Josie. "Penny is going to lead us on a "wheel-friendly" route to Soft Play!"

"Come on, you lot. Follow me!" says Penny.

"This way! Here's the sloping bit," explains Penny.

"Come on, Josie! Let's go across the car park. Soft Play is over there," says Penny.

Josie frowns. "Oh dear, what now? The buggies won't fit through the turnstile."

"Here!" Penny calls out. "There's a special sign, look!"

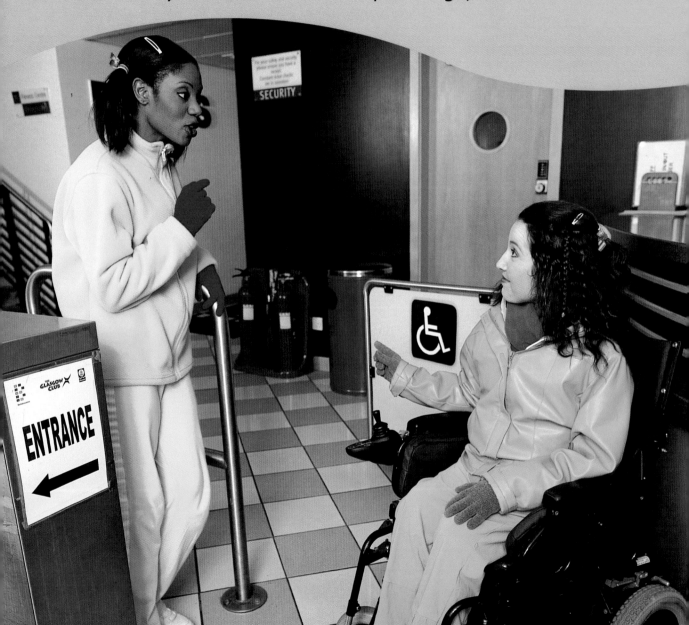

"Oh no! All those stairs!" wails Josie.

"It's OK, Josie," says Penny. "We'll use the lift, it's over there!"

They all arrive safely at Soft Play.

"This is fun, Penny!" Josie exclaims. "The toddlers are really enjoying themselves!"

"It's fantastic!" Penny agrees.

"Thanks for all your help, Penny. We'd never have got all the buggies and prams here without you!" smiles Josie.

"So, what was the story in Balamory today?"

Well, Josie was taking the Mums and Toddlers to Soft Play in the Big City, but she didn't know how to get there.

Spencer drew Josie a map, but his route meant climbing up stairs and down steep, bumpy streets, which would be impossible for the buggies and prams.

Josie needed to find a different
route. So she went to see if Pocket
and Sweet had a real map. Suzie
found a map, but it all got very
complicated, so Penny offered to
act as a "wheel-friendly" guide!

Penny's "wheel-friendly" route
was perfect for the buggies
and prams and they all arrived
safely at Soft Play.

Everyone had a
brilliant time.

"So, that was the story in Balamory! See you soon. Bye!"

BUGGIES AND PRAMS   A RED FOX BOOK 0 099 49527 9   This edition published for The Book People Ltd, Hall Wood Avenue, Haydock, St Helens, WA11 9UL
First published in 2004 in Great Britain by Red Fox, an imprint of Random House Children's Books   By arrangement with the BBC   The Book People edition published 2005

1 3 5 7 9 10 8 6 4 2

Text and illustrations © Red Fox 2004   BBC   BBC logo © BBC 1996   Balamory   Balamory logo © BBC 2002   Photographs by Nigel Robertson